NECRO SUTRA
The Compleat
Orgy

Kevin Sweeney

Black Rainbows Press

"To die in love with the carcass inanimate
To live in lust for the fetid flesh"
Gristle Licker
Cattle Decapitation

FOREWORD

WHEN I was asked to write a foreword for Kevin Sweeney's *Necro Sutra* trilogy, I thought, "Fuck that; he's not paying me, and it sounds like hard work." However, it dawned on me it would be a golden opportunity to explore one of life's "what if" moments, so I agreed.

Have I ever met Kevin Sweeney? Who knows, but let me tell you a story and see what your conclusion is.

I was born and dragged up in Greece, before my half-wit father sold the family business for a pittance and dragged us off to America. As soon as I had a chance, I headed back to Europe, and in the late 1970s ended up in Germany. Based in Berlin, I wrote filler stories for *Pochende Faust*, a soft-porn mag. My work appeared alongside articles as varied as *What's So Great About Great Danes?* through to *Clean Your Gutters*.

In 1978, my world imploded, when *Baby in a Blender* was published by *Pochende Faust*. The subsequent outcry and legal case sent me running, and I ended up in England, on the South Coast. One night, in a shitty backstreet pub, I met a young lady. She was a trainee funambulist, and whilst all indications were she had a husband, we ended up getting jiggy in the car park of a nearby scrap metal business. I saw her a few times (always, oddly, ending our secret rendezvous in the same car park), but only knew her by her circus name: Madame S.

After a few months, I headed back to the US, where I met the now former Mrs Musalata, and we made a baby: a little girl, Ophelia. Around a decade later, the former Mrs Musalata had a dental appointment, but left her purse at home. Being a good husband, I took it down to the dentist's office to make sure she could pay for her treatment, and found her butt-naked in his chair, with his cock jammed up her ass.

The divorce was acrimonious. As usual, I did what I do best, and ran away. I headed back to Europe, back to England, back to the South Coast. The only reason for my choice was the flight to Gatwick was cheap, and on arrival, I looked at a train timetable and recognized Southampton as a town I'd previously visited. Plus, I figured Ophelia - who came with me- might enjoy the seaside.

One night, in a shithole backstreet pub, I spotted a face which sparked a recognition. Behind the bar, pulling pints, was Madame S. It transpired that shortly after I left, she'd discovered she was pregnant. As a result, she ditched her life on the high wire and settled down. She gave birth to a son, a lad named Kevin. I had my suspicions but said nothing. However, when I first saw him, something smacked me in the head. He was handsome, devilishly so, just as I am, and his eyes blazed with a Mediterranean passion.

Both him and Ophelia were roughly the

same age, so I used the excuse of them being playmates to try to get Madame S back to the car park, but she wasn't having it. In truth, I was glad, because she hadn't aged that well. Kevin S spent a lot of time with Ophelia, mostly wearing her dresses and borrowing her pram and dollies so he could push it through the streets of Southampton.

I was worried about the boy, and in an attempt to set him straight, I gave him a carbon copy of a trilogy I was working on, called *Necro Fuck Frenzy*. I urged him to read it, to digest its contents, to think about another way to satisfy his lusts.

It wasn't long until I had to leave. To cut a long story short, Mr S grew increasingly irate with my interest in Madame S, so I reverted to type and ran back to America. On arrival, my luggage was lost, including my original copy of *Necro Fuck Frenzy*. My masterpiece was gone forever... although I knew a carbon copy was out there, back in England, in the hands of small boy in a dress, pushing a fucking pram of dollies around Milbrook.

So, what has this to do with Kevin Sweeney? The truth is, I'm fucked if I know!

Was the mysterious failed funambulist, Madame S, actually a certain Mrs Sweeney? I don't know. Did the young Kevin S from all those years ago grow up to become Kevin Sweeney? I cannot be certain (although he does have the look of a pram-pusher). Did *Necro Fuck Frenzy* inspire the future trilogy of *Necro Sutra*, or is all this waffle a crock of stinking horseshit? I'll tell you one thing: you ask an awful lot of fucking questions.

I can say two things with certainty. The first is Kevin Sweeney and I both share devilishly good looks and a Mediterranean gaze which makes the ladies moist at 100 yards. The second is that in *Necro Sutra*, the young Sweeney has crafted a poetic romance which weaves an unusual but intoxicating beauty. It drips carnality like bubbling fat flowing from a juicy pork chop over a BBQ. It is lip-smacking in its intensity.

I know you will enjoy the following stories, and somewhere, in the misty eroticism they evoke, I pray you find your much sought-after release.

Terry Musalata, author of BABY IN A BLENDER, THE BUTCHER AND THE BABY, and MIDGETS ON A MEATHOOK

ONE

"THE IMPORTANT thing to remember when fucking a corpse is to leave the face alone... unless you know you can get away with it, in which case you can have a lot of fun making some really cool new orifices."

He adjusted the camera, made double certain it was recording.

"Relatives might want to look upon their loved ones one last time right up until they go in the ground or the crem. If they notice that granny has an eye missing where you scooped the socket clean to fuck her in the frontal lobe, they are going to be a bit upset."

He grinned. But he was wearing a mask, which prevented his facial expression underlining his dry wit.

He glanced at the clock. He knew he was going to have to be quick. If his father caught him...

He clapped his hands together, business like.

"Okay," he told his followers. "You are watching Django Mann, the Cadaver Cassonova, and that was my top tip for neks today... but I know you don't come here just to benefit from my hard earned wisdom in the practicalities... you're here for my next few entries in the *Necro Sutra*!"

***

A whole family had come in.

A faulty boiler. No carbon monoxide alarm. Mummy, daddy, and little girl had all gone to bed and not woken up.

Silently, quietly smothered to death.

They were all flawless.

Perfect.

***

Not used to running the set-up alone, he paused the recording and double checked everything that the digital cameras were in focus and framing everything just right, that the mics were ready to pick up every pant and squelch...

He thought he heard a noise.

He stopped what he was doing and listened.

The funeral home's morgue was quiet, save for the hum of the refrigeration unit.

Was it a floorboard creak above him?

Had father got out of bed?

Listening...

Nothing else.

His heart was beating fast. It made his cock even harder.

With one last check of the equipment, he made sure his lovers were ready and got back to making the latest episode.

***

He had lost his virginity on the first day he had started work with his father.

Most people would have called it harsh for a boy of only twelve to start learning the family business, but his father thought otherwise. He even got the sign changed to reflect the future.

MANN & SON, FAMILY FUNERAL DIRECTORS: WE TAKE CARE

"That's the service we provide," said his father. "We take care. We take care for those left by taking care of those who have gone."

She had been twenty two.

A motorbike. A drunk driver.

It had been a lot of work, taking care of her; washing the limbs and face and hair, settling her features into a look of peaceful repose, dressing the body in the clothes her distraught father had selected for her.

...and late that night, after a day of taking care of her, she had taken care of him.

Young love.

***

He screwed the wrist into the vice so that the hand was held out horizontally, almost like it was ready to shake.

He fitted a hole-saw bit to the electric drill, the kind used for boring holes in wood, a cup shaped thing with saw teeth around its business edge.

He pressed it into the palm and buzzed straight through, scrims of cold flesh and jellied blood and fragments of bone spitting everywhere.

When finished, there was a ragged circular hole in the middle of the corpse's palm.

He freed his erection.

His cock was enormous, a prehistoric looking thing of bloated meat and veins and skin that looked ready to burst. It jutted up past his navel, a ferocious red tusk with a glistening purple tip.

"Entry number twenty seven in the *Necro-Sutra*," he explained, one hand wrapped around the root of his organ, the other around the cold wrist of the daddy. "The Jesus Hand Job."

He brought the holed palm down on the tip of his cock, an inch of the shiny purple helmet sticking out through the back of the hand for a moment, and then pulled the wrist downwards.

When a third of his length was through he released the wrist.

The hand was impaled on him.

He pumped his hips, letting another four inches slide up through the stigmata, one eye on the reversed view finder of the camera to check what it looked like.

"The problem with cadaver loving has always been the lack of participation from the other party," he explained. "And for the longest time something as simple as a hand job was an impossibility. But now, thanks to a little DIY stigmata, an post-mortem knuckle shuffle is entirely possible!"

He always liked to start with something a bit light hearted and fun.

***

He knew he was different, and had from time to time wondered whether his sexuality was a direct resort of the family manse and business being that of a funeral home, or if it was just good luck.

But even though he was more comfortable around the dead than the living –and certainly was only aroused by flesh in which the pulse had stilled- he found himself seemingly alone.

***

"Entry number twenty eight makes use of the hole saw once more."

Hefting the electric drill in both hands, he carefully positioned the drill bit so that the cup of the hole-saw framed the daddy's belly button. Then he pulled the trigger and bored a hole into the corpse's flabby belly. The middle-age spread jiggled crazily as the rotating saw teeth chewed in. Skin and congealed blood and streaks of yellow subcutaneous fat fanned out in a spiral across the wobbling gut.

The drill was quite hefty, and sank in right up to the chuck before he let go of the trigger and pulled it free with a small wet *pop*.

He clambered onto the gurney with the corpse, both hands wrapped around his magnificent inches.

"This one is called Up To Your Nuts In Guts!"

Using himself as a spear, he plunged his glans into the ragged hole which had once been a belly button.

He shivered.

Grinned at the camera.

"Cold!" he said. He moaned in pleasure, and sank half his cock into the corpse's intestines. "Oh yes..." Like fucking a shopping bag full of sausages. Sticky, blackish blood squirted up around his shaft.

The corpse farted.

He pounded it for a few minutes more, trying not to giggle every time decaying gas was forced out of the dry rectum.

Eventually, he pulled himself free, dragging thirteen inches of hard erectile tissue out of the corpse's belly.

The putrid blood was as good as petroleum jelly as far as lubrication went, and he kept himself at full mast by squeezing and rubbing his colossal cock as he addressed the cameras once more.

"And then we immediately go into entry number twenty nine in the *Necro-Sutra!*"

With his free hand, he made a spear point with all his fingers and plunged them into the gaping wound. Once in, he rummaged around until he was able to get a firm grasp, and then pulled out a length of greasy, purplish intestine.

He hauled out a foot length of cold and slippery digestive tract, then another, then another. He kept tugging it out and laying it in coils on the corpse's crotch like it was rope, and then when he had enough, he suddenly looped a length of it over his head and woun it around his neck.

And pulled tight.

He struggled for breath. His eyes bulged.

He kept wanking.

"Number twenty nine," he wheezed. "Auto-Erotic Entrail Asphyxiation!"

Choking himself with the daddy's intestines, he furiously masturbated.

When he came he nearly passed out.

Thick ribbons of ivory coloured semen squirted from the gasping slit of his glans, jetting into the air and coming apart to fall like fat pearls all over the morgue floor.

***

Pornhub, MyDirtyHobby, MommysGirl, Mofos Network, RedTube, TeamSkeet, Lucy-V, Dog Fart Network, TSplayground, The White Boxxx, DesiPapa, YouPorn, 21Sextury, Brazzers, Chaturbate, XNXX, MrSkin, Round And Brown, BimBim, CumPets, AuntJudys, Oye Loca, Shop Lyfter, Digital Playground, SexAlArab, Her Limit, WhyNotBi, SeanCody, xHamster...

A thousand others.

It seemed every kind of copulation, every kink, combination, or colouring of carnality had terabytes of content freely available on the internet... except his.

Even people who fantasised fucking cartoon characters had communities.

***

He used his other arm to lift the corpse from the gurney, cradling it awkwardly until he was able to manoeuvre it around so that it was facing the camera.

The little girl had a heart shaped black mole at the corner of her mouth. Her glazed eyes were open, gazing into forever, and her blonde hair was limp across her forehead.

Her mouth opened.

Bloody fingers wiggled out from between her lips.

Hello!

He had turned the corpse into a puppet.

He tucked his fingers back behind her lips, dragged the body across to his crotch, and gripped his black-blood slicked cock with the grotesquely distended mouth.

He wanked himself hard and fast. The girl's hair flopped and flipped as her face ran up and down his thick shaft like it was a giant meat-harmonica.

Just as he was about to blow his muck, he cupped the bell end with her mouth.

He ejaculated.

Semen blasted from the corpse's nostrils like she had a heavy cold and was blowing her nose clear of snot.

***

He found the dark web.

He found Circles, the social network for the deranged, demented, and depraved.

He found his tribe.

It wasn't long before he became an active participant and a rising star. He called himself Django Man, started his own circle, and became an underground sensation as he shared his many lonely years of experimentation, practical guidance, wisdom, insight, and personal list of special moves with a small but hungry group of fellow ghouls.

The *Necro-Sutra* videos blew up.

***

When he had framed the mummy's pregnant belly just right he thought he heard another noise above him, in the flat above the funeral home.

He froze.

Listened.

The noise did not repeat.

Still...

Maybe it would be wisest to stop her for the night. Tidy up and make good, like nothing had happened.

His father couldn't catch him like this...

He strained to hear any tiny indication that the old man was moving about up there.

Nothing.

Probably just turned over in bed, flipped the pillow to the cool side and settled down into the next REM cycle...

Anyway, he was too excited to stop.

Number thirty one was too rare an opportunity to pass up.

Even after coming so many times already, his enormous dick was still rock hard and ready to go. It was twitching with his heart beat.

He bowed to the camera.

"Position number thirty one in the *Necro Sutra*," he explained, his tremulous voice betraying his excitement. "The Matryoshka!"

He produced a trimming knife as if from thin air, the kind with a segmented blade that you slid up by pushing in a button in the handle. He extended it by two segments.

He started just above the neatly trimmed triangle of her dark brown pubic hair, sliced open the skin all the way up to her navel. Yellow subcutaneous fat glistened in the wound.

He repeated the cut, slicing through the thin layer of insulation to reveal the weave of muscles beneath.

Once more he cut, digging deeper and having to put some effort into it this third time, almost sawing through the tougher material.

Decaying blood oozed like sap as she began to part.

What was revealed in the gash underneath the harsh fluorescent light was something semi-translucent.

Discarding the blade momentarily, he dug his fingers into each edge of the huge wound and pulled it apart, unveiling what was within.

It was a sac of membranes with a curled up passenger, almost like a grub curled within a rotten fruit.

He picked up the blade.

Split the distended womb.

He put the knife down again. It clattered off the edge of the gurney onto the floor, but he wasn't paying any attention.

He turned back to the camera.

"Matryoshka," he said, his voice quivering with excitement. "Or as we call them, Russian dolls!"

He gripped himself around the root and clambered onto the gurney.

Strictly speaking it would have been better if the foetus had been female, but beggars couldn't be choosers.

He sighed as he sank in, as if he were lowering a body weary with a day's work into a hot bath.

Cold. Slimy.

Gorgeous.

He shivered with pleasure.

And then he got down to business.

The camera framed the scene perfectly... including the door ten feet behind the action, which suddenly opened just as he climaxed.

The gentlemen framed by backlight flooding in from the funeral home's back corridor looked like an older, wearier version of the gentlemen skewering what was on the gurney, except his grey hair was not immaculately swept back but looked tousled as if he had just got out of bed.

The son froze in mid thrust.

The father gazed in shock at the scene before him.

The shock metamorphosed into rage.

"What. The. Fuck. Are. You. *Doing?*"

Each word was bitten off, every syllable of the rhetorical question hard and hateful.

The son gaped.

He struggled to get upright, onto his knees.

His crotch reared.

The thing shish-kebabbed on him waved its arms as if it were alive, though even if had been alive it couldn't have cried out... not with its mouth crammed so full its cheeks had split all the way to the ears.

"I..." he said, but the words died between his brain and his tongue. He looked down. He gulped, licked his lips, and tried again. "I can explain."

His father's eyes narrowed.

"You can explain?" he asked. "You can *explain? Explain?*"

He punched the door frame.

And he roared

"*YOU   KNOW   I   HATE   SLOPPY SECONDS!*"

TWO

THE BABY'S corpse was hanging from a hook which was supposed to suspend bunches of bananas.

The idea was that the ethyl gas the yellow fruit release as they mature wouldn't cause other nearby fruit to ripen too quickly if they were kept separate. People don't realise that bananas are the main cause for their fruit bowls blooming into glorious rot before time.

The banana suspending device was a kitchen gadget he had picked up in IKEA. It was about the same size and shape as a desk lamp, only instead of a hooded bulb it had the hook.

When he bought it he was not thinking about hanging fruit from it, but rather this alternative purpose. He had had to sharpen the end of the hook in order to pierce it under the baby's spine between its thumb nail sized shoulder blades so that it would hang down ready for milking.

He slid a measuring jug under the dangling body. The dead infant's arms and legs hung around the round mouth of the jug, its swollen chest directly above.

The baby was male. Its eyes were closed.

He checked his close work set-up. The three cameras he was using to record were all good to go, ready to start recording simultaneously; one was focussed on the hanging baby corpse, another was turned on a large saucepan of boiling water on the electric stove, and the third took in the wider work space he would be utilising, with its stainless steel sink and draining boards and the various knives he was going to use.

There was a separate set-up with two other cameras for when he was demonstrating what all the hard work was leading up to, both cameras focussed on a camp bed against the far wall of the kitchen. The light was dim, the walls bare red bricks, windows draped with heavy black curtains. The only sign of individuality was a ceramic vase from the Moche culture of seventh century Peru displayed on one end of the kitchen countertop, depicting a woman masturbating a male skeleton.

Satisfied, he ran through his script in his head and pulled on his mask. The mask was a standard gimp mask with slit eyes and a zippered mouth. The only unusual thing about it was its colouration; instead of being black or red, it was blue, with a white square around the nose.

He pressed record, and allowed five seconds of dead air before he began.

"Hello and welcome once again my dear chums." His voice was rich and plummy and too English to be anything but an accent put on for effect. "It is I, your dear friend Blue Peter! I am so pleased you have decided to join my Circle again... and though I can use from previous editions of my little program that our viewership has increased, it is still quite a lonely looking number! Oh, there are so few of us, aren't there? And fewer every day!"

Blue Peter paused.

Solemn.

"I am of course referring to the loss of one of the leading lights of our benighted community, Django Mann, to whom this episode is dedicated. Django was an inspiration to so many of us, especially myself... as thanatophiles, we know what it is to be alone, truly alone, and by being a such a bold and effective champion of our cause Django gathered many of us to him like moths to a flame, and we found ourselves to be, perhaps, not so lonely..."

Another pause.

"A brief biographical moment, if you will indulge me; it was Django's instructional programs on the practicalities of corpse-coitus that first gave me the courage to admit to what and who I am, as well as the tools I needed to pursue my sexuality, and thus to eventually develop this, my own Circle dedicated to the more esoteric aspects of cracking open a cold one. And from thence, I have come to know all of you, so that I can truly say I am no longer quite so alone..."

Blue Peter wiped a tear from the eye slit of his mask.

A beat.

"We owe the cadaver Casanova much."

Then he clapped his hands briskly together, all stiff upper lip and ready to get on with business.

"Now, what are we about today? Well, how about a quick review of some of the areas we have covered so far...?"

***

The stages of decomposition roughly correspond to the main branches of necrophiliac sexuality, and it is important to understand the subtle differences between.

Not all necrophiles are attracted to all corpses. Did you really think that? That's offensive! Educate yourself. I'm literally shaking.

We don't just say that someone is a homosexual, after all; we acknowledge that a gay man may be a bottom or a top, or may have a particularly preference for a body type, such as a bear, or a chub, or a twink.

Ahem.

After death, when bacteria and natural processes begin the process of rotting, a body goes through certain stages. First there is bloat; the flesh swells with gasses, features are distended, skin is waxy, and bodily fluids become "frothy". At this point a body can be seen as perhaps being a bit chubby and fun, and certainly capable of making the most varied range of noises as the anaerobic generated gasses and rotting blood/spinal fluid/stomach acids are forced through decaying inner chambers to squelch, gasp, fart, and even groan sensually. At this stage a corpse is closest to imitating the state of being alive, in much the same way as highly detailed sex dolls can mimic living behaviour, although with different scents and flavours.

Next comes active decay. This is the point where a body experiences its greatest loss of mass as more complex necrophages move in to continue the work that the bacteria have already begun. Flies lay their eggs, maggots hatch, and the body becomes a frenzy of activity as the spawn feed and a general purging of fluids into the surrounding area. Many corpse-fuckers enjoy this stage of decomposition owing to the fact that orifices (anus, eye sockets, etc) are filled with moving bodies (maggots, worms, beetles etc.) which affords unique sensations to sexual organs introduced into these cavities full of corruption. At this stage also, the smells of decay are strongest, as well as the flavours of decaying bodily fluids. A body in the active decay phase can be left in place to generate a cadaver decomposition island (CDI) which many find a comforting, moist embrace. The end of active decay is normally signalled by complete disintegration of the soft tissues and the migration of the various pupas.

Finally, there is the final stage known as dry remains, which amongst the various sub-sexualities of necrophilia has the least number of admirers... having said which, it is to these people that Blue Peter is directing his lesson today.

Yes, there are people who are sexually attracted to skeletons. Who the fuck are you to judge?

***

"Now, some of you are probably wondering why I've chosen to use a baby for today's tutorial, so let me assure you now, it's simply a matter of practicality, NOT perversion! I am NOT a kiddie fiddler and the fact that I am going to fuck it is purely because it is dead, and NOT because it is a baby!"

Behind his mask we must imagine Blue Peter looked offended at the very suggestion.

Then he shrugged.

"Although I must admit, there was an opportunity inherent in the choice that I simply could let slip past... hence my improvised milking rig."

Blue Peter crouched down behind the suspended infant corpse, hands folded.

"The fact is, when I went about sourcing today's specimen I learned a very curious medical fact... it seems that galactorrhea occurs in around five percent of neonates, which makes it quite rare and quite wonderful! That is to say, as a result of the mother's hormones floating around in the baby's blood stream, the baby itself can start producing breast milk, which in pre-enlightened times was called witches milk, as it was thought to be a sign of demonic influence!"

Blue Peter pointed at the dead baby's chest. The tiny nipples are quite swollen.

"Now, as we all know, the necrophile's watch-word is opportunity...so even though today's program is about dry remains and the various applications they have, how could I let this pass by?"

And so saying, he reached under the corpse and used his thumb and forefinger on each hand to grab the tits of the dead child, before gently squeezing and pulling at the same time as if he were milking a cow... and sure enough, material squirted forth, material that was less milk than yoghurt, or possibly even the kind of pus that a teenager squeezes from a zit, thick and sticky and off-white.

The curdled milk spurted into the measuring jug below like an old man spunking, intermittent and foul, the very last dregs of semen left in withered testicles.

Blue Peter milked until nothing more would come out.

"Well, there you go! Witches milk!" he said. He picked up the jug and dipped his nose in, sniffing. "Hmmm, passed its use by date, but still an opportunity I couldn't let pass!"

He set the jug to one side.

"We'll come back to that in a little bit, but now we should get on with what we're here for... harvesting a skeleton."

He tugged the dead baby off the hooks, splitting the skin of its back with two soft noises like rotten silk being torn.

Blue Peter held the corpse up by gripping its ankles with one hand and letting it dangle head downwards, much like he was displaying a fish he had caught.

"The first thing you'll need is a large saucepan full of boiling water. Of course, if you're going to use a full size adult to harvest from, you'll need to divide the body up into portions small enough to fit... if you need help with the dismemberment, just check out my previous video, 'Proper Disposal: Grinding Up Corpses After Grinding On Corpses', for full details."

Blue Peter was now in front of the saucepan of boiling water.

He held the baby's head above the surface of the bubbling liquid.

"Now I cannot stress enough, *lower* your body into the water do NOT drop it! Dropping it risks splashing, and scalds are not fun! Safety first, friends!"

And so saying, Blue Peter slowly dipped the baby face first into the saucepan. He gently released the ankles and the sad little corpse slipped beneath the heaving liquid.

It began to bob, a hand or a foot occasionally breaking surface as the dead baby twisted and turned on the bubbles.

"Now, in order to fully boil off all the meat and fat and muscle, as well as the internal organs, you're going to need a few hours of constant heat, skimming waste material from the top as and when. This is time consuming, and I'm not going to spend this whole video watching a boiling pot... in fact, we can move right on, because here's one I prepared earlier!"

Blue Peter bent down out of sight, only to straighten up again bearing a silver tray on which was arranged the skeleton of a dead infant, and a tall plastic cylinder filled with...stuff.

This second item looked uncannily like the old fashioned dessert known as a Knickerbocker Glory, a mixture of different ice creams and sauces and chopped nuts.

"It was twins!" he announced.

He reached under the counter again to retrieve a box shaped chunk of black metal with dials on it. This he placed next to the cylinder of stuff.

"Now, before we get down to the meat of the matter and have ourselves some fun with these bones, I'd like to refer you back to the issue of *disposal.* If you're familiar with the history of our fellow ghost-riders, most of them were caught when trying to dispose of the remains of their lovers; Dennis Neilson favoured flushing them down to the toilet, and was found out when he blocked the drains, whilst Ed Gein," Blue Peter paused to hold a hand over his heart when saying the sacred name, as any Born A-Gein necrophile would, "made lampshades and clothing out of the evidence, which later was used to convict him."

Blue Peter unzipped the mouth of his mask.

"So what should you do with the muck and muscle that you've boiled off your bones? Well, as long time viewers know, I prefer the Dahmer method of disposal!"

The contents of the tall plastic cylinder are not melted blobs of vanilla and banana flavoured ice cream layered and streaked with strawberry sauce, but are in fact the cooled and partially solidified remains of boiled baby, fat and sinew and organs. Something like a tiny mask –a face without eyes or teeth- was squished up against the side, its boneless nose a pig snout against the clear plastic.

There was tiny kidney on the very top, where the cherry should have been.

Blue Peter picked it up and fixed it on top of the thing with dials, and with both parts together it became obvious that it is, in fact, a blender.

He placed the lid on the top and flicked a switch. Instantly, the contents began to whir as the blades of the device rapidly began to liquefy the chunky contents of boiled baby flesh.

When it reached a smooth milkshake like consistency the colour of cooked salmon, Blue Peter switched the blender off, removed the lid, and picked up the plastic cylinder with one hand.

He raised it to the camera-

"Cheers!"

-and began to drink the contents.

Runnels of blended fat, blood, and guts ran down either side of his zippered mouth, dripping onto the counter.

When half of it was gone, he lowered the concoction and burped. A thin layer remained on the upper lip of his mask like a pink moustache.

Wiping his mask clean with the back of one hand, he held aloft a single finger with his other.

"Just to make it clear, I am aware that a baby in a blender is a cliché."

He clapped twice, a physical segue.

"Okie dokie artichokie, onto the main event!"

***

You do know you don't have to go any further, don't you?

So you were interested in the whispers about what was on the dark web, interested enough to download the relevant software to get on there. But that doesn't mean you can't stop right now, turn away.

You found Circles. You had heard of it, the so-called Facebook slash TikTok of the internet's underbelly, a social network for sociopaths. A place where monsters congregate, offer services, wallow, boast, posting pictures and videos of the atrocities which are their existences upon this planet of the damned.

You trawled around for a bit. Clicked on this Circle, scrolled through the feed, watched clips, deciphered the slang and shibboleths of a world you never knew existed and were INITIATED.

Clicked another Circle.

Grew sick.

Fascinated.

Clicked.

Eyes widened.

The word "No" a whisper on your lips as you saw that yes, it was, yes, these things were really happening to people...

Clicked.

(Felt a part of you -a very important part of you- die.)

But you still have a choice.

You can click OUT. Close down the program that lets you doom-scroll through this earthly circle of Hell.

You can save yourself.

Look away now.

Go on; leave.

...

No?

...suit yourself.

You had your chance.

***

A close up shot of a long but skinny cock, with pubic hair curling on the shaft almost all the way to the peeled back foreskin.

Blue Peter gripped his erection with one hand and pointed the purple bell of the glans towards the camera. By squeezing gently with his thumb and forefinger, he made slit of the urethra gape.

"I must admit, I got the idea for this from a book," he said. "It's called *Damnation 101,* and it's a thumping good read about a school in Hell where they train demons how to torture people."

He was sitting on a high stool, his leather trousers dropped to his spread thighs.

A bowl on the counter to his right held what at first glance could have been big white match sticks without the brown tips that are used to strike them alight.

"I'm going to assume that my male viewers are all going to be familiar with the practice of urethral sounding, but if there are any of you who don't know what that is, it's the practice of inserting things down the eye of your todger in order to stimulate sexual pleasure. You can buy glass or metal rods, or even pour fluid down there... but remember what I said about improvisation?"

He picked up one of the baby fingers from the bowl between his thumb and fore finger and pushed it down into his piss tube.

He shivered.

"Oooo WOW!"

With his left hand he stroked his cock in long gliding motions, massaging the tiny bone load downwards, like somebody force feeding a goose millet in order to make *foie gras*.

Then he plucked another bone from the counter and pushed that one into his urethra, following the first, and massaged it down his length again.

He repeated this five times, until the final bone stuck halfway out of his glans.

"Now that's what I call a *boner*!"

Blue Peter gave his pale, skinny erection two gently pumps. The bone in the end was sucked in and then stuck halfway out again, a surreal snake tongue tasting the air.

Shivering with pleasure, he restrained himself.

He reached over the counter, out of the camera shot, and returned with the skull of the dead baby clutched in his free hand.

He held it up to the camera.

"Now here's a fun fact; did you know that you are born with both sets of your teeth already inside your head? First your baby teeth will emerge, one by one, up until about the age of three, and you'll have those until at around about six or seven you shed those and your adult teeth start pushing out! Looks weird, doesn't it?"

The skull was grinning with two rows of teeth, one above the other.

"Now, I bet your thinking that I'm going to go for a blow job... but you'd be quite wrong! No, because here's another interesting fact about infant bones; they don't fully fuse until you are about half a year old, which means you have these two soft spots on the skull called fontanels that are quite soft, a small one towards the back and a larger one towards the front."

Blue Peter turned the skull around to show the areas he was talking about.

"This is *very* useful, because as we gents all know, none of us are quite the same dimensions, so no matter how girthy or not you might be, you'll be able to make a glory hole just the right size for you!"

So saying, Blue Peter held the skull in his hand in just such a way that he was able to press his thumb securely against the small fontanel at the back of the skull. Gripping tightly, he pressed down hard and it popped inwards like the plastic-foil seal on a bottle of multi-vitamins.

He inverted the skull and positioned it over his finger-bone stuffed erection.

He grinned a trifle sheepishly.

"Another small confession and I do hope you'll all forgive me, but... well, I got the idea for fucking a skull in this fashion from yet *another* book, called *The Shopping List*."

And so saying he slid his skinny hardon into the hole he had made and fed his cock all the way through until his glans –still sporting its white tongue of bone- emerged from between the jaws that sported double rows of teeth.

He worked it up and down, gently and slowly rocking his hips. The tight ring of neonatal skull plates gripped his shaft just firmly enough to make his eyes close in pleasure.

His glans poked in and out of the dead infant's mouth like it was blowing a raspberry at the world.

"Hmmmm..."

Blue Peter's eyes popped open, startled from his reverie by remembrance that he had an audience.

"Ah, ahem! Yes! Where was I?"

He snapped his fingers.

"That's right! I forgot the milk!"

Reaching off camera again, he brought the jug from earlier back into play, the jug full of what was once superstitiously known as witch's milk.

There was an off-white stick protruding from it. He used this to stir the mixture, which had begun to separate into a thin yellowish fluid and thick creamy curds; he stirred it vigorously to mix the two elements together again, and then withdrew the stick to reveal that it was in fact a baby's thigh bone.

Blue Peter stood up from off the stool, letting his leather trousers fall down further.

"Waste not, want not," he told the camera, holding up the thigh bone that was thickly coated with cheesy colostrum which dribbled down its length and over his knuckles. "Whilst almost any bodily fluid will make an adequate lubricant in a pinch –I know my first fantasies were fuelled by a palm full of phlegm- it is indeed a rare treat to be able to fuck one's arse using such an uncommon unguent!"

And so saying, with one hand still wrapped around the skull that his phalange stuffed stiffy was impaled upon, he turned in profile to the camera so that his viewers could witness him force the human-dairy greased infant femur into his rectum, groaning with pleasure as he did so.

When the ball joint of the thigh bone pressed up against his prostate, he slowly pulled the length back out again, at the same time shoving his hips forward to force his erection up into the skull.

Blue Peter began to saw back and forth, back and forth, the femur gliding into his puckering sphincter as he withdrew his shaft through the fontanel, then reversing direction so the thigh bone eased out of his guts like a hard white shit as his boner boned the baby's brain case.

He began to speed up, keeping the rhythm but increasing the tempo as he moaned in ecstasy, reaming out his rectum and headfucking simultaneously, faster and faster, only pausing once or twice to dip the femur back into the witch's milk before ramming it back up his shit chute.

But of course, nothing good lasts forever.

Blue Peter had trained himself, and even lost in the throes of corpse-coitus as he was he did not neglect to angle his groin back towards the camera when he felt his orgasm threatening, and when it reached its crescendo...

"*YeeeeeeAAAAHHHHH   FUCK YESSSSSS...*"

He jammed himself up to the hilt in the baby's skull, his glans breaking off three of its teeth with his final hard thrust as he ejaculated, the force of his spunk shooting the finger bones out of his urethra like Hell's own tracer bullets, each with trailing a comet tail of semen.

One even hit the camera lens. It made a *plink* sound and left a smear and later, editing the footage, he could barely believe his luck.

He couldn't have choreographed that better if he'd tried.

Panting, getting his breath back, Blue Peter looked at the camera even as his cock wilted between twin rows of teeth.

He thanked his viewers, reminded them to subscribe if they hadn't already, and promised to read every comment.

***

His numbers were insane.

Blue Peter sat back in his ergonomic office chair, the fake leather wheezing as he pushed back from the figures on the screen.

He had five times the views of all his previous necrophilia themed videos combined.

He'd gone viral.

All because...

Well, it wasn't because it was dry remains, was it? He couldn't kid himself about that. Ghouls who were into bones were a niche kink within an already niche sexuality.

No.

It wasn't because it was dry remains.

It was the source of the bones.

Babies.

Blue Peter had a strange thought. Or at least, the thought was strange given the context; the context being who and what he was.

There are some sick cunts out there...

He stared at the numbers.

Those were numbers you could monetize.

Those were Django Mann numbers.

He licked his lips.

Babies... but getting...

There was a knock at his bedroom door.

The young man who called himself Blue Peter on the dark web's premier social network closed his laptop.

"Yeah?" he called.

The door opened.

His mother smiled in at him.

"I was just nipping out to the shopping," she told him. "Any special requests for dinner? How about your favourite, toad-in-the-hole?"

When he didn't answer immediately she looked more closely at his face, and frowned in concern.

"What's the matter, son? Don't you feel well?"

Blue Peter licked his lips.

Those numbers...

"Mummy," he said.

"Yes?"

"I..."

She waited.

He sighed.

"I've just checked my ratings. They're... unbelievable. Through the roof. But if I'm going to follow them up I'm going to need more of the same kind of content."

He licked his lips again.

"I need another baby," he told her.

Her frown deepened. She gave the matter some thought... but not too much.

She'd never been able to say no to him.

"Well, okay," she said. "The shops don't close for another hour, we can have a quick fuck now, and then again after I get your dinner ready. But... won't you lose viewers if they have to wait nine months for new content?"

Blue Peter shrugged, picking up his video camera.

"That's okay, mummy, incest is really popular too."

His mother shook her head, already unbuttoning her blouse.

"There are some sick cunts out there," she sighed, closing the door behind her.

THREE

I DON'T think it will ever cease to amaze me that people want this depraved, disgusting, deranged SHIT... but who am I to argue, if this is what the public demands?

And of course, it had made him a very wealthy man.

Got to remember to call mum when we land...

The plane began its final descent.

India.

The first stop on Blue Peter's world tour, travelling the globe to further the cause of necrophilia... and though he still hadn't settled on a name for the new series, he was leaning heavily towards calling it *TOMB RAPER.*

***

"At some point during a cremation, the meat is perfectly cooked."

The camera is zoomed in close to Blue Peter's masked face. The camera work is shaky, wobbling as it pans back to fully encompass the scene.

Blue Peter is wearing a strange silver bodysuit and his trademark gimp mask, which is entirely blue except for a square of white in the middle. He isn't alone; another figure, also wearing an all encompassing silver body suit, is stood to his side. This second figure does not wear a gimp mask to protect his identity. He is an Indian gentleman of indeterminate age, his face smeared with grey ash, his hair dusted with the same smoky dust.

Both of them are standing next to a burning funeral pyre on the banks of a river. It is early evening, the setting sun turning the polluted waters the colour of decaying blood.

The pyre is occupied.

Blue Peter places a friendly, silver gloved hand on the Indian man's shiny shoulder.

"Hello subscribers! Blue Peter here for the first stop of my world tour series of videos exploring necrophilia around the globe! I'm here on the banks of the Ganges river in India for a traditional Hindu *mukghani*, or cremation ritual! For today's act of charnal carnality I've enlisted local necrosexual Uppaluri! Say hi to the subscribers, Upp!"

The Indian gentleman grins and waves a silver gloved hand.

"Greetings, my friends!"

Blue Peter laughs.

"Smashing! Now, Upp here is a member of the Aghori sect of Hinduism, who practice a number of unorthodox religious practices that they believe will help them escape from the cycle of reincarnation... for instance, living in charnal grounds, adorning their bodies with the ashes of the dead, crafting jewellery from bones, and even cannibalism! Supposedly, by violating the illusions of socially constructed taboos they seek to obtain a realisation of the self's identity with the absolute..."

Blue Peter pauses for effect.

"Because, of course."

He laughs again.

"Anyway...I bet you're wondering about the

fancy clobber we're both wearing, right?"

A pause, as if waiting for a reaction; *yes Blue Peter, we certainly are wondering that! Pray tell!*

He runs his silver gloved hands up and down the shiny surface of his bulky body suit.

"These are most commonly known as fire proximity suits, worn by fire fighters and volcanologists to protect themselves from incredibly high temperatures! The particular kind me and Upp are wearing are technically fire entry suits, made from vermiculite and able to withstand ambient heat up to two-thousand degrees Fahrenheit! But some of the more observant of you have probably already clocked that I've had these suits tailored since I got them..."

Blue Peter uses one gloved hand to grip a trunk that sticks out of the front of the fire entry suit at crotch level, a trunk made out of the same flame resistant material as the rest of the outfit.

And he begins to wank it.

Uppaluri, taking his cue, similarly begins to masturbate the shiny silver hose that his cock is sheathed in.

And both begin to stiffen.

Blue Peter sniffs the air extravagantly.

His stomach rumbles.

"Hmmmm... you know, I think she's almost done! Upp, as my guest, I'll let you choose; arsehole or appetite?"

The Aghori *saddhu* grins wider.

"Thank you kindly, my friend! I think I should like... the appetite!"

Blue Peter nods.

Then both men, taking long, astronaut-on-the-moon sort of strides, wades into the flames of the funeral pyre, huge silver books crunching through the charring wood pile.

The body in the middle of it has turned black. It's impossible to tell what gender it was.

But of course, when it comes to corpse-copulation, what flavour it was in life is irrelevant; only the fact that it doesn't have a pulse matters.

Uppaluri is at the head end. With bulky awkward fingers he prises the cadaver's mouth open, causing its cheeks to split right back to the burnt stumpsof its ears, and eases his silver sheathed stiffy between its jaws.

Meanwhile, Blue Peter has grabbed its legs and forced them apart. Where he grips it tight, the blackened skin slides away on a layer of bubbling fat, exposing cooked muscle underneath. There is a meaty ripping sound, an amplified version of the noise a chicken leg makes when it is pulled off a freshly roasted bird, and then he has access to the anus which is dribbling with hot spitting juices; he grips his vermiculite wrapped erection by the root and guides himself into the steaming rectum.

"Woooo!" he cries. "Wow! Ooooo! Even in these suits, that's a tad warm!"

The flames of the fire lick around the men and the body, and the two living members of the *ménage a trios* are both visibly sweating.

"Yes, warm!" agrees Uppaluri. "But nice, most nice!"

And then they begin to fuck it, sawing back

and forth in rhythm, the charred body being alternately pushed and pulled through the burning pile of wood.

The camera operator is doing their best to keep everything in frame, but it's not easy, as the heat haze from the holy inferno is making it hard for the auto-focus.

But the picture is clear enough when Uppaluri and Blue Peter both, on an agreed upon signal, stop porking the meat and tilt their groins back to *lift* the charred corpse off the pile of burning wood for a moment, speared as it is through its mouth and anus on their hard cocks.

"Check it out!"cries Blue Peter in triumph. "Now THAT'S what I call a SPIT ROAST!"

And the corpse's perfectly cooked buttocks slip off the bones of its arse and plop sizzling into the fire.

***

Hi mum it's me...

Yes I'm in India I...

Yes, I know, I'm sorry I didn't call earlier, it's just been such a rush, and everything is so mental here!

Hmm?

No, I've not been having any drinks with ice in, you warned me about that about a million times before...

Yes, I'm eating properly; they have McDonald's over here, but they don't sell burgers so I'm on McNuggets for breakfast, lunch, and din...

Because cows are sacred, so they don't eat them...

Well I don't know, maybe one of their Gods is a cow, they've got like a hundred different ones...

Listen, the first shoot went really well, I got some excellent stuff, I'll be editing the video and uploading it tonight...

No, I've got all the encryption software I need and I'm using an untraceable IP; I have done this before! I'll send you a copy, I jus...

Hmm?

Oh yes, of course the heat suit worked! I'd be in the serious burns ward of some smelly local hospital otherwise, wouldn't? I...

Yes, but of course you can't see the cum shot because of the suit, but yeah, I fucked the arse off it... literally!

Anyway, how are you doing? Weren't you supposed to go in for a scan today?

Really?

So everything's okay, it's healthy?

You know what I mean, at your age complications are more...

You know why! I've got to keep providing content or interest will slack off! I wish I didn't have to leave you there on your own but...

Oh for fucks sake... listen, I've got an early flight tomorrow and I've got to get the new video uploaded tonight so I'm hanging up now...

Of course I love you.

Yes.

Yes.

...of course I'd rather be in your bed!

I'm doing this for us, you know that.
Right.
Yes.
Right.
Mum, I'm going now...
Mum...
Yes, I love you too, okay...
Bye mum...
Bye!

***

Branding was everything, which was why Blue Peter had his own range of prophylactics for the discriminating corpse fucker.

They were, in fact, what had made his fortune.

Though his videos of funereal-fornication were rampantly popular on the web's premier social media site, Circles, it wasn't like YouTube or Tik Tok or Only Fans; monetisation was much trickier. If you wanted to make some serious crypto-currency you had to get creative.

And so he had.

Blue Peter had a loyal following of necrosexuals world-wide, all of whom he knew had money to spend, and a terrible secret they kept from the vanilla world; the average ghoul tended to hide behind a "normal" existence, including living lovers, spouses, and families, much in the way that homosexuals used to present as "breeders" when the law was still oppressing them. A life pretending that the breathing, sweating, *warm* flesh society expected you to pork turned you on when all you truly desired was cold, clammy, and silent.

Then one day, he happened to read an article about the history of the humble rubber johnny, and had a light bulb moment when it mentioned that the earliest examples were simply lengths of animal intestines tied off at one end...

He made the first few batches himself at home, and then when orders started coming in faster than he and his mother could handle he out-sourced production to China, via a contact he made on Circles. And thanks to that country's high-turnover of executed political dissidents, there was a steady supply of human intestines to feed demand.

The advert played before every new uploaded video;

"Do you suffer with ED because your lover isn't RIP? Does their pulse re-pulse you? Can you only get a stiffy for a stiff? Well never fear, you're old mate Blue Peter has the solution!"

The genius of it was quite simple; by using a contraceptive sheath made from the intestinal tract of a dead man, a lasting erection was achievable with which one could plumb the anus, vagina, or oral vault of a living human *without them ever knowing*.

The world tour was in fact entirely funded by sales of Blue Peter brand *Necronomicondoms*!

***

Hi mum, it's me, I've arrived at...
Hmm?

Well I'm sorry to hear that, of course I am, but what can I do about it? I can hardly massage them from the other side of the world!

America.

Yes, America.

I did tell you!

Yes, I did!

No, I told you I couldn't leave you all the details; what if the authorities showed up or something, with a warrant to search?

No, of course they won't! I told you, everything is encrypted, airtight!

I'm just saying IF THEY DID turn up, they wouldn't be able to track me down, not without a paper trail...

They won't!

I just meant, IF THEY DID.

They won't!

Look, we're just going round in circles here...

Trust me!

Anyway, back to what you said before... if your feet are really that swollen, just go to the doctor...

Hmm?

The same thing happened when you had me?

Okay...

Okay...

Same cravings? What cravings?

Really?

Sardines and Mars bars? Together?

...and brown sauce?

That's sick!

No, that's really gross! Oh god, it's making me feel queasy thinking about it! Sardine and Mars bar sandwiches with brown sauce, I mean...

Hmm?

Yeah, we're shooting the next one tomorrow. Yeah.

I am a bit worried, but I've got that tube of Deep Heat you bought for me to rub on my cock afterward.

Yes, I'll think of you when I'm applying it!

Yeah, you know you're the only warm one for me.

...you know I'm thinking of you when I stick it in!

Bad girl!

Okay, well I've got to get an early night. You should too, you need the rest.

Yeah.

I love you too mum.

...okay, yeah...

Right.

Okay.

Bye mum.

***

"So, Dr Blank, I guess my first question has to be; do you have Walt Disney here?"

The man with the paper bag on his head chuckles, and the eyes visible in the holes he has cut for vision seem to sparkle.

"Y'know Pete, that's a common myth right there! Walt Disney was never cryogenically preserved at all!"

"No?" asks Blue Peter, clearly disappointed.

Dr Blank shakes his head with a rustle.

"No sir! Walt was cremated, and his ashes interred at Forest Lawn Memorial Park in Glendale!"

Blue Peter turns to the camera, head tilted to one side, fists planted on his hips.*Would you BELIEVE it?*

"Bugger!" he says. "I was really looking forward to getting a blow job from the man behind the mouse!"

Dr Blank chuckles again, and glances shyly at the camera.

"Y'know Pete, we should really get a move on," he whispers. "If these folks are out for too long they're gonna start thawing..."

Blue Peter nods.

"Right!"

The camera pans back from the shot which captures both men from the chest up to reveal more of them –Dr Blank in a lab coat and nothing else, Blue Peter in a leather vest, similarly *sans* clothes from the belly down- as well as the room and the thing on the floor between them.

The room is white and sterile and full of high-tech equipment. A freezing mist spilling from an open storage unit swirls around at ankle height. The thing between the two necrosexuals looks like a totem pole, though rather than have each face turned in the same direction, they alternate; the one at the bottom, stacked on a stool, is facing left, with the one sat on top of it facing right, the one atop that facing left, the next one right, the next left, and the final one right.

Each has had their mouths forced open. Their eyes are wide but glazed over with a film of ice, and frost coats their cheeks and hair.

"For the next stop on my world tour, I'm at a cryogenics laboratory somewhere in the USA! I have to keep it a bit vague, because my mate Dr Blank here (who you might guess does *not* have Blank as his surname on his birth certificate) would lose his job if his employer ever got wind of what the good doctor gets up to on those occasions he does a bit of *over time*."

Dr Blank chuckles.

"They'd can my ass for sure!"

Blue Peter grips his long, veiny erection by the root.

"Shall we?" he asks.

"You betcha!" replies the anonymous doctor, wielding his own pork sword.

The reason for the faces on the faux-totem pole being twisted alternately left and right now becomes obvious; it's so each man has an equal number of holes to pole.

Blue Peter slips himself between the pale blue lips of a woman in her late seventies.

He yips.

"YAAA! Oh, fuck me, that's a bit bracing! Jesus, I like 'em cold, but mate, that's something else!"

Dr Blank just shudders a little as he stuffs his stiffy into the mouth of a man with a walrus moustache, the hairs of which sparkle with defrosting ice.

"*Unnnhh...* you get used to it Pete!"

Blue Peter relaxes a little, and begins to buck his hips, his cock sliding back and forth over a tongue that feels like ice cream, his shaft slipping across lips like chunks of ice.

He's beginning to enjoy it.

He pulls his cock out and selects the next face up the pole on his side, a face so wrinkled with age that it's hard to say if it was a man or a woman. But it has a nice tight mouth, so who cares?

The skin of the tiny wrinkly lips split when he forces his inches in.

Over the top of the totem pole, Blue Peter asks, "So how does cryogenic suspension cost then?"

Dr Blank vigorously pumps the moustached face before also selecting another face to fuck, and only answers when he gets a good rhythm going.

The totem pole wobbles dangerously. Both men grip a set of ears each to keep it in place.

"Good question Pete," grunts Dr Blank between thrust, thrust, thrust. "Full body cryopreservation will cost you anywhere upwards of $200,000, but if.... *unnnhh...* if you're on a budget we can do a neuro for only... only $80,000."

"A neuro?" wonders Blue Peter, pumping.

Dr Blank gasps.

"That's what we call a decapitation Pete! Hence our... hence our... friends here!"

Blue Peter pulls his erection out of the wrinkly face and stands on tip toes to spear the final one on his side, a rather attractive blonde who is staring into eternity.

Dr Blank's paper bag is getting soggy with the sweat of his exertions, but he too opts to swap for a new orifice.

Both men are now fucking as hard and as fast as they can, cocks sawing inside dead mouths full of frozen saliva, ball sacks slapping against chins like blocks of ice.

Blue Peter comes first.

He roars and slams himself up to the root in the dead blonde's face, his pelvis mashing her nose flat with a *crunch* and seconds later twin runners of semen are flowing from her squashed nostrils like snot.

He staggers back from the tottering totem pole, the blonde's face still impaled on his throbbing erection as the rest of the pile collapses, leaving Dr Blank dry humping the air.

Blue Peter turns to the camera, wrapping his fingers in the girl's crispy hair, pulling her off his sagging hardon and holding her aloft like a trophy

"Now THAT'S what I call getting some HEAD!" he roars.

***

The world tour was more than just an excuse to get away from his mum for a few months, it was a righteous crusade.

The success of his necronomicondoms had been a surprise, but it just went to show the sheer number of people with a nek fetish who there were out there, a silent minority who were romantically inclined towards the other "silent minority."

Why should loving the dead be considered a crime? Who did it hurt, really? Wasn't love, as the poets and greeting cards had it, eternal? Did it not transcend this mortal coil? Why should it be "'til death do us part", particularly if being a member of the "choir invisible" was exactly the quality that you were attracted to?

It incensed him. The sheer injustice!

Look at history; King Herod had sex with his wife for seven years after her death; Herodotus wrote of Periander fucking his wife's corpse, that he "baked his bread in a cold oven"; the Xianbei emperor Murong Xi had intercourse with his empress as she lay cold in her coffin!

It was in art, in everything from the epic *Orlando Innamorato* by Matteo Maria Boiardo through to *Romeo & Juliet*... to quote the Bard;

> "Shall I believe,
> That unsubstantial death is amorous,
> And that lean abhorred monster keeps
> Thee here in dark to be his paramour?"

Call it *unnatural*? Then look to the *natural* world where so-called "Davian behaviour" has been observed in ducks, penguins, sea lions, pilot whales, rock doves, cliff swallows, leopard lizards, garter snakes, crayfish...all of them willing to fuck a corpse of one of their own species!

Necrophilia was as much a legitimate sexual orientation as being a breeder, or an ace, or a kiddy fiddler. It was nothing to be ashamed of... no, the opposite in fact! There were pride parades each year in cities on every continent, gays and lesbians and queers, drag queens and drag kings, gym bunnies and bears and twinks in leather and denim waving rainbow flags; Blue Peter had visions of his people openly celebrating who they were with processions of hearses, dressed in shrouds and waving the skull and cross bones.

They should rise up and make themselves heard!

And Blue Peter was just insane enough to think he could be the figurehead for such a revolution in psychosexual politics, the Ghandi of ghouls, the Messiah of *morgue amour*.

Hence the world tour.

Thanks to Circles, he had contacts everywhere.

The videos that Blue Peter uploaded to Circles of his travels to all four corners of the earth to witness, record, and indulge in necrosexual practices were intended to stand as a manifesto of the movement he wished to foster.

***

Hello?

Blue Peter. Order number 734286544.

Read back the details to me, I don't want any mistakes.

Right.

Right.

Yes, she's my mother. What of it?

Of course I'm sure. I thought you were a

professional?
Yeah?
You've been paid, you have your orders.
Yes, this is my confirmation; do it.

***

A montage of scenes from other entries in the *Tomb Raper* series...

IRAN

Atop a "Tower of Silence", a stone platform built for the practice of sky burial, where bodies are left in the open air to naturally decay and be devoured by birds.

There is a central pit towards which the cobbled floor of the tower's upper level slopes, allowing decomposing material to naturally sluice away. Arranged in radiating rings around this pit are the bodies. The innermost ring are dead children, the wider ring around them is made of woman, and the outermost ring is men.

The bodies are in various states of decomposition, bloated with the gases of corruption, writhing with maggots, or bones upon which only fragments of flesh remain. Everywhere there are birds, mainly corvids and vultures, dipping their beaks into faces to sip liquefying brains, guzzling greasy green ropes of intestines like worms, pulling off decaying testicles and labias swarming with insect larvae.

So many grins turned up to a faded blue forever overhead. The ancient cobbled stones are slick with the juices of decay and bird shit, the scavengers crapping out the digested muscle of the deceased onto their own bleaching bones.

The birds are undisturbed by Blue Peter as he selects a partner, or at least, a part of a partner; the carcass snaps at the spine when he embraces it, the entire upper torso collapsing to the ground as if sawn in half, leaving him only the partially skeletonised legs and pelvis.

It's more than enough.

He lubricates his cock with a fistful of black and white guano and sticks it into the decaying folds of the cunt. His glans can be seen in the open abdominal vault, bobbing up and down in the remains of the womb.

He reaches down into the rotting remains of the reproductive system and squeezes the worm riddled flesh around his dick, and so becomes one of the few human's in history who has ever had a wank during full vaginal penetration.

PERU

"When you think of mummies, you think of Egypt," Blue Peter says, holding up the dried and sere body of an alien baby. "But it has actually been a common practice all over the world for thousands of years."

The infant couldn't have been more than a year old when it died. Its skin is tight on the bones, the skin paper thin and brown with age.

"This is an example from the Collagua tribe of south-eastern Peru, who were active about seven hundred years ago."

He holds the mummified child's head close to the camera. The skull is deformed into a sort of traffic cone shape, making it certainly *look* alien.

Blue Peter has a squirty bottle of baby oil to hand, which he squirts along the length of his erection.

"As you can see, the Collagua people practiced artificial cranial deformation. The skulls of newborns are still very pliable, and by binding them tightly with cloths and wooden boards the bones can be shaped into an elongated tear drop shape. Apparently it was a status symbol, though of course crushing the brain like that would often result in death."

Blue Peter squeezes a liberal amount of baby oil over the mummy's disturbingly pointed head.

And then, masturbating with his other hand, he forces it up his arse just like any other butt plug.

PAPUA NEW GUINEA

Blue Peter was in luck for this one; a land developer had been trying to clear the tribe from this area of the jungle for years so that they could plant a palm oil plantation here. He made a deal to bring in a small group of mercenaries he'd contacted on Circles to massacre the stone-age people.

A tribe who still practice the funerary rite of cannibalising their loved ones upon death.

They caught them in the middle of the feast.

Afterwards, Blue Peter and his camera crew waded amongst the bullet riddled bodies to find the chief; as leader, it was his honour to ingest the brains of the deceased.

After a few strokes with a machete, Blue Peter has hacked open the man's belly. The stomach full of chewed up neural tissue is still warm when he sinks his cock into it.

JAPAN

The body drops.

The rope tightens.

There is short, sharp *crack*.

For maybe ninety seconds the condemned man's feet dance upon the air.

And then death.

The body sways gently on the end of the rope.

Blue Peter was surprised that Japan even had capital punishment; he was doubly surprised when it turned out that they used hanging as the chosen method of annihilation; he was *triply* surprised at how easy it was to gain access to the event.

But then, as has already been noted, there are necrophiles everywhere, in every walk of life from concert pianist to police officer. And wasn't it natural that they should be attracted to certain professions? Funeral director, morgue attendant...

Executioner.

The momentum of the corpse slows, slows... stops.

But the body is not entirely still.

The dead man's prison issued uniform trousers stir at the crotch.

In a voice over to be added later, Blue Peter will remark upon this well known phenomena, observed in hangings since time immemorial, known by the wonderful euphemism as *angel lust*.

The sudden damage to the spinal cord and the restriction of the major arteries causing tumescence in the very recently departed.

The dead man has a hardon.

Blue Peter is very quick in approaching the body, and just before he pulls its trousers down, he undoes his belt and lets his own pair of stylish olive green chinos drop to the floor.

Carefully, he presents his rear, and backs up onto the dead man's rigid cock.

He butts up against it.

The body swings back a little, and then it swings back again. The cock slides into Blue Peter's gaping anus.

By carefully shoving back at regular intervals, the corpse is a pendulum, swinging back and forth, and the dead man fucks him.

***

It has been an exhausting nine months, but he makes it home in time for the birth.

His mum is huge, her belly swollen to enormous size.

He's just in time.

In every great movement there are martyrs.

This is what he tells himself, tears in his eyes, as he switches the camera on.

He's a little worried about the sound quality

with the vast numbers of flies buzzing in the air, so he is careful to speak louder than he normally would.

"Welcome once again, my friends," he says, speaking to camera. He has a tissue to hand, to dab at his eyes within the zippered sockets of his gimp mask. "And though I might be crying, please be assured at just how happy I am to have you here for this very, *very* special episode."

He folds his hands before him, and takes a deep breath.

"You and I have been on such a journey together! You have followed me all over this dying Earth as I have sought to explore the full limits of our tragically misunderstood lifestyle! And I hope that you have not only taken solace in knowing that you are not alone, that there are in fact thousands, *tens of thousands* of us fellow necrosexuals to be found on every continent and in every walk of life... not just solace, but inspiration!"

He nods slowly.

"And our love is just as valid, just as varied, just as virtuous as any other! We see beauty where others see ugliness; we find joy where others only know despair. We find passion in the burying grounds, and ecstasy within mausoleums."

Blue Peter sighs, reminiscing over his many adventures.

"I wanted to end this series with something special. These past nine months I have travelled far and wide to record every form of nercosexual love possible. I have pushed charnel carnality to its absolute limits. It would seem that there is nowhere else to go."

He turns to look at his mother lying on their bed, the vast dome of her belly an eclipse. The skin is so distended that it is almost transparent, the skeins of blood vessels visible through the stretched epidermis.

Her flesh has a greenish tint to it. The bed clothes are soaked with post-mortem fluids. But there are no signs of violence; when he gave the hit man his orders, he was quite clear that she was not to suffer.

"But there is one death phenomena left to encounter. One of the rarest."

He stands next to his mother's corpse, and lays his hand on her vast belly, stuffed to bursting with rot.

"If a pregnant woman dies, naturally the life she is carrying will die with her... but, thanks to the build up of internal gasses, it is still entirely possibly for her to give birth, as those gasses can, under the right circumstances, force the dead foetus out of the womb. This is called a *coffin birth*."

Blue Peter places both his hands on his mother's stomach, lacing his fingers together as if about to give CPR, and pushes down hard.

The corpse queefs.

The farting sound of escaping air is shockingly loud, though brief, as it is soon replaced by a much wetter noise as her water's break and a gallon of decaying amniotic slime gushes from her fungus-furry cunt, soaking the already sticky bed. The stuff is as thick as curdled semen, and stinks like rotting eggs and corrupted fish and the juices in the bottom of a sanitary bin stuffed with discarded tampons. It overflows the bed, dribbling to the floor in thick, snotty rivulets.

And then something the size of a fist squeezes from between the cunt flaps encrusted with dead thrush.

It slips out and spins lazily in the puddle of gunge between the mottled thighs.

Blue Peter picks it up gently.

So small. Only half developed.

It looks melted.

He impales it, his cock splitting the tiny anus and snapping its pelvis in two, surging up through its body to force its semi-liquefied insides out of its mouth, spongy lungs and heart and liver and wormy intestines erupting from its mouth in a foaming volcano just before the shaft of his penis bloats out the throat and then the swollen purple glans of his penis bursts through the fontanel in the top of the skull like a chick breaking free from within an egg.

And then he bends over.

This is a trick he has not showcased before, but one that he has worked on since his adolescence.

Blue Peter can suck his own cock.

Bending at the waist, his mouth engulfs the tip of his penis and then his lips smoothly slide over the foetus's ruptured skull, so that the entire head bulges his cheeks apart.

He jerks his hips. One thrust.

One thrust, but so exquisite that Blue Peter comes at once, shooting ivory ribbons of spunk and brains into his own throat.

He bites down on the foetus's throat.

Chomps.

He straightens up and spits the things head and a large portion of his own cock onto his mother's deflating stomach.

It lands with a sad little splat right on her navel.

Perfect.

It's time.

The gun was hidden just off camera.

Blue Peter slides the barrel between his teeth, aims it straight upwards, and pulls the trigger.

***

"What a mess."

"Jesus..."

"You ever seen anything like this?" asks PC McHardy.

"No. Never," says PC Hawker. "Well, not *exactly* like this. Looks a bit like munging, don't it?"

PC McHardy nods thoughtfully. The similarity is apparent.

Both men remove their hats in an act of deepest respect.

"Well... I suppose... last wishes and all that."

"Yeah. It's what he would've wanted."

"Is that camera still going?"

"Uhhh, yeah. Yeah it is."

"Well then..."

The hole in the top of the gimp mask is

exactly the right size.

   The inside of the skull is still warm.

   Neither uses their finger to determine this.

THE END

AFTERWORD

Necro Sutra was originally a story I wrote as a response to a tale written by Simon McHardy and Sean Hawker called "Munging", which they dedicated to myself and Peter McCaffrey. It was supposed to be a bit of fun, as well as offering a little background on a character that appeared in my serialised novel *The SeVIIn Sick Sins*.

But then it took off.

What happened was, a Tik Tok book reviewer called Juan G. Vizcarra reviewed my story on his Spanish language channel, and within weeks that review had over a million views. Suddenly, thanks to Juan, I had a following in Latin-America, and I was being asked for more stories set in the depraved world of *Necro Sutra*.

So I wrote another story, aiming to be even more horrendous than the first... and then, because I felt I had to bring it all to some sort of conclusion, I wrote a third part... which you can see brought the whole thing around in a circle, back to the original inspiration.

I've included two bonus stories here that have similar themes, I feel.

Kevin Sweeney

PHANTOM COCK SYNDROME

"PHANTOM cock syndrome," she repeated.

The prostitute was staring at the mass of scar tissue between his legs. It was well healed, but it still looked like dozens of wads of used chewing gum squashed together.

"The fuck are you talking about?"

He sighed. He was lying on the hotel bed with his hands laced behind his head, waiting patiently whilst she had removed his trousers and boxers to find... nothing.

Well, not what she had expected anyway.

"Look, a lot of times when people have limbs removed, like a hand, or a whole arm, or a leg, because they've been in a horrible accident or it's cancerous, they can still feel the missing bit. Like, their foot might have been amputated because of frost bite, but years later they can still feel it get itchy. Phantom limb syndrome."

Her look of disgust mixed with confusion moved back and forth from his face to his crotch.

"Yeah," she said uncertainly. "Yeah, I think I did 'ear about summink like that."

"Right. Well, that's what I've got, only it's a phantom cock. And it's not itchy, it's rock bloody hard and I need to empty my phantom balls."

"So 'ow did you lose your meat and two veg then?"

He shrugged.

"I'm Jewish. When I was circumcised, nobody knew that the *mohel* performing the ritual had a cannibalism fetish, so when it came to the *metsitzah b'peh* –that's when they use their mouth to suck blood away from the cut- he kind of freaked out and ended up eating my genitals."

He shrugged again.

"Guess that's how I got hung up on an oral fixation!"

She asked the obvious question.

"Are you taking the piss?"

"Only through my catheter. I carry it around like a little metal drinking straw. See the hole? I stick it in there, like piercing the top of a fruit juice carton."

There was a small hole in the middle of the twisted pucker between his legs.

"So, what, you want me to stick my finger in it or summink?"

"No, I want a blow-job, just as we agreed."

"But there's nothing to suck on."

"I disagree. I can feel that I have a very hard erection, and my balls are aching."

"So... you want me to pretend?"

One hand came from behind his head and see-sawed in the air.

"It's real to me, so it should be just as real to you."

"And you're going to pay me?"

"Of course."

She didn't have to think about it for long; a pretend BJ for the same cash she'd get for sticking an actual rotten, smelly cock in her mouth?

She went to work sucking and stroking on the empty air between his thighs.

He sighed, and occasionally gave her instructions, like explaining it was a lot longer and thicker than she was giving him credit for. The word "horse" was used.

She rolled her eyes but started using both hands as well as her mouth. She even gagged a little.

He moaned and groaned and told her harder, deeper, yes, that was it, keep doing that... Her head began to hammer up and down like a machine piston.

Then he roared and came.

Her mouth was suddenly full of cold, cold slime, so much so that she gasped and jerked backwards, gagging for real.

He was gripping the pillows on either side of his head whilst a massive column of ivory gunge jetted from an invisible point a foot above his ruined crotch.

One of his hands suddenly grasped the nothing and twisted, and the jet started splattering her face, coating her cheeks and eyebrows and lips in a substance that she was very familiar with, though not in such quantity or such coldness.

When it was over, he lay gasping and she was knelt there dripping.

"What the fuck was that?" she asked eventually.

He grinned, still breathing heavily.

"Phantom cock spunk," he told her. "Erectoplasm!"

THE BEAST WITH TWO BACKS, FIVE CUNTS, AND A THIRTY-SIX INCH PENIS WITH SEVERED BABY ARMS SEWN ONTO IT TO MAKE IT LOOK LIKE A CENTIPEDE

FRANKENSTEIN'S CREATION thought of itself as Adam, and three hundred years after entering exile in the wastelands of the Arctic circle, Adam returned to a much-changed world.

During his absence, a zombie apocalypse had ravaged the planet.

None left were living. All he met were shambling corpses, searching for hot brains and steaming guts. Of all the things stumbling about the wasteland of civilisation that had been dead, only Adam was capable of rational thought, yet he was left unmolested, as the corpse-things instinctively recognised him as of their creed.

The ruins fascinated Adam.

Before the end, when humanity died screaming between the jaws of the ever-swelling population of ghouls, civilisation had advanced in ways he could never have dreamed of, not through all those endless nights alone beneath the auroras. The cities were full of towers that rivalled the Biblical Babel, and the roads were choked with the rusting hulks of carriages that required no horses.

By deduction, some curious vehicles he saw destroyed in fields or smashed into buildings, must have been capable of flight. Flight!

Inside many buildings he found furnishings and devices whose essence eluded him, such as strange boxes of glass and an unknown material, filled with glittering, intricate innards. When he discovered an extant library, he set to the task of making sense of the world he had missed in exile, and learned the names of these objects; computers, tablets, laptops, mobile phones, televisions... The workings of these things seemed as magic to him, though he knew it was merely natural philosophy, or, as the art had come to be called, science.

His interest in this technology was quickened by learning that the humans had used the truly miraculous engines for what was a singular purpose, as an access to "the internet", a sort of subtle body of knowledge much like a library, but seemingly given a primacy of purpose for the collection and distribution of pornographic material.

He attempted to use some of the intact devices, but without the vitalizing force of electricity, none had responded to his ministrations.

Adam gave up on physicks and turned instead to that branch of natural philosophy of which he himself was a walking masterpiece, biology.

He had not come out of the Arctic seeking human *companionship* after all.

Adam's centuries of solitude had not been monastic in nature. He was a living creature, and he had the needs of all life. He filled his belly with fish and crustaceans caught from the icy waters and had spent his nights with only his imagination for company as he indulged in onanism. He had, in fact, crafted entire igloos from the frozen product of his self-abuse, his colossal priapic member -sewn together from a half dozen different donors- shooting reproductive fluid into the sub-zero air where it instantly froze into ivory beads that he collected for construction.

His imagination was provided by the lobes of at least three different minds crammed into his huge skull, two male and one female, accessing the memories of long dead strangers and their romantic dalliances, but even so, it had eventually run dry.

His thoughts as he had trudged back out of the wastes had been on warm flesh. To find only decaying meat had been a disappointment, and the knowledge that he had just missed mankind's greatest achievement... that the humans had created a repository for the accumulated filth of aeons, accessible to all, whenever and wherever they wished...

It was too much.

He had left the library and had gone on a rampage, tackling any zombie he came across, and raping them to twitching pieces. He collected the pieces he most enjoyed and stuffed them into shopping carts he lashed together with chains into a train, and eventually, after a day and night of killing the dead he had sufficient parts to begin.

Adam had secured medical texts.

He had all the time in the world.

His initial creations were clumsy but effective. His brain was not only male, and so he favoured both kinds of reproductive organs. The first members of his harem were not beautiful, mere masses of sutured flesh with numerous orifices or jutting members into and onto which he would insert or impale himself and slake his lust.

As the decades past he gained skill with needle and thread, and found new ways to reconfigure the putrid yet curiously *not* putrefying meat of the zombies. He journeyed far and wide, an ever growing stable of fuck-things trailing in his wake.

He created a centaur-thing that bore semblance to several different quadrupeds; it had udders, for example, fashioned from numerous breasts stitched together. It also had antlers made of cocks. He made a stable for it and shared its bedding after sessions of playing the beast with five backs.

He made something like the totem poles favoured by Native Americans, a thing of heads stacked one atop the other. He would start in one mouth and move to another, his lust demanding a change in texture; he would stuff himself into a face that had tongues fused together like a starfish, and later, after changing faces half a dozen times, would finish in a head he had crafted with a triple row of teeth.

He created Brides... he created Husbands. In Adam's eyes they were beautiful, crafted using only the most attractive parts he found; a head claimed in the Baltics, a torso from the Balearics, a cunt from

Krakow, a cock from Kiev.

Sometimes, rarely, he found survivors.

He was a gentleman, offering them the chance to join with him and his army of lovers.

He was shot at, threatened with flames.

Mostly, the survivors did not survive. They died screaming in pain when they could have gone howling in ecstasy.

Centuries passed, and so Frankenstein's creation united the whole world in peace and love... and sutures.

Printed in Dunstable, United Kingdom